My Best Friend Is Ariel

By Lisa Ann Marsoli
Illustrated by the Disney Storybook Artists

Random House 🏠 New York

Copyright © 2006 Disney Enterprises, Inc. All rights reserved. Published in the United States
by Random House Children's Books, a division of Random House, Inc., New York, in conjunction
with Disney Enterprises, Inc.
RANDOM HOUSE and the Random House colophon are registered trademarks of Random House, Inc.
Library of Congress Control Number: 2005928294
ISBN: 0-7364-2388-5
www.randomhouse.com/kids/disney
MANUFACTURED IN CHINA   10 9 8 7 6 5

"May I have your attention, please?" Sebastian the crab tapped his baton on the podium to start the rehearsal. The undersea symphony was preparing a special birthday performance for King Triton.

Sebastian raised his baton, and the musicians began to play. Beautiful music filled the sea, until—*CLANG!*

"Who dropped that?" Sebastian demanded.

"Um . . . I did," said a timid voice.

"Not again, Coral!" cried Sebastian. "The best way to play the cymbals is to HOLD ON TO THE CYMBALS!"

"Yes, sir," Coral answered, her cheeks red with embarrassment.

The rehearsal went from bad to worse. Over and over, Coral missed her cue. Then she dropped her cymbals again. Then she tripped and landed on top of a kettledrum.

Sebastian threw down his baton. "Rehearsal is OVER!" he fumed as he stormed off.

Ariel hurried over to help Coral. "Don't mind Sebastian," she said. "He just wants everything to be perfect."

"I've never been good at anything—let alone perfect," Coral replied.

"The only thing I'm perfect at is making Sebastian mad!" Ariel told her with a laugh. "You should have seen his face the last time I went up to the surface!"

"You've been to the surface?" Coral said, amazed. "Wow! You must be the bravest mermaid ever!"

Ariel laughed. "I don't know about brave. It's just something I like to do that's different." She took Coral's hand. "I have a special place where I keep all my found treasures. Would you like to come see it?"

"I'd love to!" Coral exclaimed as she waved to her brothers and sisters.

The two mermaids swam to Ariel's secret grotto. Along the way, they met up with Flounder.

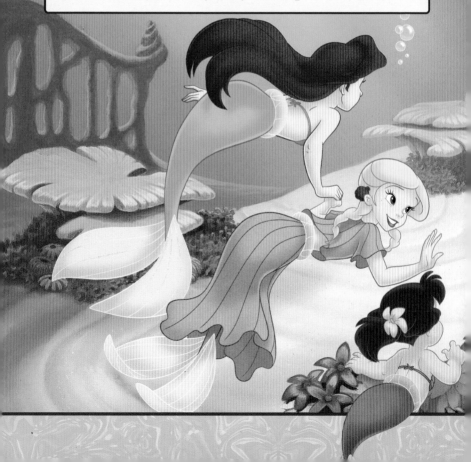

Coral's eyes widened when they arrived at the grotto. She swam around the cavern, admiring the beautiful jewelry and trinkets. "Where did you find all this?" she asked Ariel.

"I found some at the bottom of the ocean," Ariel answered.

"And in sunken ships," Flounder added.

"You've been inside a sunken ship?" Coral gasped. "Weren't you scared?"

"Not really. Were you scared, Flounder?" Ariel teased.

"Nothing to it!" Flounder fibbed.

"So what are we waiting for?" asked Ariel. "Let's go!"

Coral and Flounder trailed behind Ariel as she swam. Soon they arrived at a ship resting on the ocean floor.

"Come on!" said Ariel, disappearing through a small porthole.

"She wants us to follow her in *there*?" Coral exclaimed in disbelief.

"Yup," answered Flounder. "And the sooner we do, the sooner we can leave!"

When Coral and Flounder found Ariel, she was going through the contents of an old steamer trunk.

"Look at this!" said Ariel, holding up a purple parasol.

"And this!" Coral exclaimed, picking up a fancy lampshade. "I wonder what it's for."

"My friend Scuttle can tell us," Ariel said. "Follow me!"

Soon Coral found herself swimming up, up, up to the surface.

Before she had time to be scared, the friends had arrived at the rock where Scuttle was perched.

Scuttle examined their treasures. "That's a scribbleflow," he said, looking at Ariel's parasol. "Small humans use it to ride around in the ocean."

Then he turned his attention to Coral's lampshade. "Oh!" he said with excitement. "That's a fancy outfit human ladies wear on special occasions."

As they headed home, Coral asked Ariel if she could keep the lampshade at the grotto. "It might get lost or broken at home," she explained.

"Of course," Ariel agreed. "The grotto is my secret place, and it can be yours, too."

A few days later, when Ariel swam up to the grotto, she heard the most beautiful singing.

"Coral!" Ariel cried. "I didn't know you could sing like that!"

"I can't really," said Coral. "Not like you."

"Nonsense! You have a lovely voice!" Ariel declared. "You should be singing at my father's birthday concert, not playing the cymbals."

The little blond mermaid shrugged. "I just like singing to myself," she explained.

The next day, Sebastian made Ariel and the orchestra rehearse over and over again, but something seemed to go wrong each time.

"The big day is tomorrow!" the crab said, fretting. "This concert must be fit for a king! Now, let's try it again."

By the end of the rehearsal, everyone was exhausted—and Ariel's throat was sore.

The next morning, Ariel could only whisper.

"Laryngitis!" wailed Sebastian. "Oh, no! Now who's going to sing the solo?"

Ariel led Sebastian to the grotto, where Coral was singing. As soon as Sebastian heard her, he asked Coral to take Ariel's place.

"Me?" Coral said. "But I can't!"

"You must!" Sebastian insisted. "Otherwise, King Triton's birthday celebration will be ruined!"

Ariel and Sebastian hurried Coral back to the band shell.

"You shouldn't let being scared stop you from doing things," Flounder told her.

Coral thought about the great, scary things she had done recently—visiting a sunken ship and going to the surface—all because of Ariel. Now her new friend was counting on her.

"All right," Coral said slowly. "I'll do it."

That night, when Coral peeked out from backstage, she nearly fainted. The entire kingdom was in the audience! And there, sitting in the royal box, were King Triton and Ariel.

Coral took a deep breath and swam onstage. As the orchestra began to play, Coral started to sing softly. But as her confidence grew, she sang more loudly, her voice filled with joy. Before she knew it, the concert was over, and the audience erupted into applause!

"Coral," said Sebastian, smiling broadly, "you can give away your cymbals. From now on, I'm making you a court singer!"

After the show, Ariel found Coral backstage with her family.

"I didn't know you could sing like that," gushed one of Coral's sisters.

"Ariel believed in me, and that helped me believe in myself," replied Coral. She turned to the princess. "Thank you!"

Ariel still couldn't speak, but she smiled at Coral and gave her a big hug. To the young mermaid, it was worth more than a thousand words.